Prologue

When the world was young, man set sail on the ship of time. Buffeted for 700,000 years by the wind of change, he eventually evolved into a single species, *homo sapiens*.

Around 8,000 years ago Neolithic man began recording significant headway. He learned to write, he trained the barnyard animals, he invented pottery, giving rise to the world's *true* oldest profession, and somewhere along the way he realised he was not alone, that he shared his natural world with supernatural spirits.

The gods were delighted – man took note and celebrated this theophany at Knossos on the isle of Crete, home of the Goddess Ariadne, guardian of the gates of time. At Knossos the gods fashioned a divine plan which, man willing, would lead the spirit-alloyed species to maturity. Thereafter, God and man could work together in familial harmony, jointly determining and co-creating the future.

Goddess Ariadne of Minoan civilization

All things considered, it was a rather simple plan. The Dagda, the Divine Father, would warm up to the Southern Semites and ordain a series of covenants with his new friends. Later, His Divine Son would take human form and through His Resurrection offer His Father's promises to all mankind. (This came to be known as the New Covenant.)

Danu, the Divine Mother, for her part would work quietly in *mystery and moonlight*. Her eternal nurturing would foster greater understanding and co-operation between mankind and the gods, and herald the first new cultural cycle for man in 8,000 years.

Tuatha Dé Danaan: People of the Goddess Danu. The Celts

The Divine Mother and Ariadne moved north. Soon after, the peaceful matrilineal culture of Crete ended. Danu entreated a people who, unlike the Southern Semites, did not write their history, preferring instead the tradition of oral truth.

As their plan unfolded, the gods empathetically allowed strife to push their chosen peoples in both the north and the south into the margins of society. Their grand design required such 'remnant flocks' who remained steadfastly devoted both to the gods and to the old Neolithic values: open spaces; streams with fish; trees with birds; wild animals; friends, and the responsibilities of family and freedom. Then like a thief in the night, the day came.

Ariadne acquired a good ship. From the Celtic Otherworld, the gods summoned a doughty pirate captain with unique skills. And an angel disguised as a prophet travelled to a small village in Celtic Cornwall to call a young lad to his rendezvous with destiny.

After 8,000 years, the Stone Age was *finally* coming to a close.

1 The Pirate

Beltane, AD 2000
SOMEWHERE IN THE CELTIC SEA

Sam Bellamy looked in his handy mirror and admired the sartorial elegance of its reflection. It returned the confidence he invited, for it isn't every day that a sailor from Plymouth (UK) calls on a Graeco-Celtic goddess, or any goddess for that matter. He wanted, indeed he needed, to look his Sunday best.

One final glance. Well, he had aged a trifle during these last 274 years, if ageing is the correct word, but he looked gentlemanly, proper enough he told himself to meet a goddess, and briefly tidied the cockade in his signature tricorn hat. "Mustn't keep milady waiting," he mused, as the sweet shrill of the bosun's pipes heralded his arrival aboard the *Numinous*.

Captain Samuel Bellamy died at sea in 1717

The gallant captain strutted through the entry port, choosing to ignore the side boy's white gloved hands. "Greetings, Captain. Her Ladyship sends her compliments and will see you straight away, sir," announced Benson, Ariadne's flag lieutenant. "This way, sir."

The *Numinous* was stunning, a Celtic Otherworld flagship fit for a goddess, no doubt. Square-rigged at nearly 1,000 tons she was Bristol-built around 1850. Bellamy secretly admired her gleaming white decks which seemed almost translucent, bathed by the light of May's full moon.

Ariadne waited on her quarter deck. "Good evening, Captain, welcome aboard. I am Ariadne of Delos," she said, extending her hand. "I trust your short journey in our launch was not in the least unpleasant."

"Delightful, Milady, and I am as pleased to meet you as I was surprised to be piped aboard, and humbly honoured on both accounts," responded Bellamy, punctuating his charm with a polite, temperate bow. Humility had always parted his lips reluctantly, but he surprised himself with this meagre, albeit acceptable effort. Two centuries of humbling 'Otherworldly' work was paying off, no doubt about that either.

"Lord Nelson insisted on adding the pipes when he reformed the Otherworld's Navy some years after Trafalgar. Our dear admiral is well on his way to becoming a god, you know."

Lord Horatio Nelson, hero of the Battle of Trafalgar

It was in all the papers, so of course he knew. He cautiously crafted his reply.

"Seamen the world over have the greatest respect for him, Milady. I myself served in Blake's Navy sixty years before Lord Nelson. Afterwards, I removed to New Plymouth in the Colonies in search of . . . freedom." Ariadne covered her mouth. For a moment it occurred to Bellamy that he may have ventured too far; that his unstudied, casual tone was inappropriate; his unbridled honesty too direct.

"It was your destiny to do so, my good Captain, and is the reason I have invited you here tonight."

The invitation, he recalled, read more like an order than an option, and offered precious little detail of this mysterious 'mission' being proffered. All he ever wanted from life was freedom – a ship to sail; other ships to capture and take as prizes. In two years he became one of the most successful pirates in history, then he died into obscurity, so the goddess's use of this word 'destiny' intrigued him.

"Shall we adjourn to the ward room, Captain," she continued. "My officers have prepared a thorough briefing for you." She held forth, Bellamy thought, more like an admiral than a goddess; not the deportment he had expected.

Dinner followed the briefing after which Ariadne turned her attention from the group as a whole to Bellamy. "You've met 'Flags', Captain, so with your permission I should like him to join us for a whisky. As he will be first lieutenant on your new ship, there remain several matters you two should discuss."

'Flags' – the universal, impersonal moniker for an admiral's flag lieutenant

Bellamy rendered an unnecessary, assenting nod as her staff officers retired. He had correctly guessed during the presentation that the goddess herself would appoint his ship's company, and

Benson certainly had seemed both competent and knowledgeable during the course of the evening. So he was pleased. Lord Nelson, on the other hand, would have had to rely upon press gangs to round up the needed men for His Britannic Majesty's ships. For his part Bellamy had wanted to be a sailor all his life and had joined the Navy in 1701 at the age of 12, same age as Nelson; and so loved the Navy that he could never quite accept that press gangs were necessary, same sentiment as Nelson.

"Gentlemen, now that we are alone let us speak of destiny – yours in particular, Captain Bellamy." He was all ears. "You are a gifted sailor and would certainly have received your flag had you remained in the Old World. But as an adventurer, risk taker and natural born leader, you became impatient, intolerant of events which veered in unanticipated, yet ultimately useful directions."

Aah! *His* deportment was under scrutiny. Also, she was veering her remarks uncomfortably close to home. Her charges were true enough but difficult to hear, none the less. Plus there was a sub-ordinate in the room who, too, was all ears. Even the notion of sub-ordination did not go well with him. Pirates (*un-marqued privateers* in Bellamy's parlance) were all equals, able to vote their captains in or out of office. That was freedom!

"Destiny, Captain, always veers. It never travels in a straight line and often continues beyond the grave. Nelson's destiny was *both* Trafalgar *and* Trafalgar Square, and quite possibly even greater glory than that. Had you survived that Cape Cod storm in 1726 you would have been hanged for piracy. Not much destiny there, is there, Captain Bellamy? Even Cotton Mather could not have saved you."

Now there was a name he hated. Bellamy had no use for the self-righteous Puritan, nor any other men of that ilk.

"So, we saved you Captain. And now we need your skill, your courage and your faith in the resurrection of which you spoke so often and so convincingly to your mates. Successfully navigate the next storm, Captain, and the gates of time shall open and close on your command. The gods are with you. This is your destiny!

"Benson, I would be most appreciative if you would kindly escort

Privateers carried 'letters of marque' issued by warring nations authorizing the capture of ships the good Captain to his quarters. Your new ship, *Mystic Rose*, arrives on the morning watch, gentlemen, so make some decisions fast."

2 The Angel

Sunday, 16th July, 2000
ST. BURYAN, CORNWALL

Tobit's granny lives alone in a medieval Cornish cottage nestled into the pretty Lamorna Valley, a brisk walk from St Buryan village. Consisting of a modest manor house and several outbuildings, the property was divided years ago into smaller estates including hers. Her picturesque cottage is surrounded by lovely gardens and a pond. It also serves as her studio. The Lady of the Manor (Granny's oft-used phrase) writes children's stories, sculpts, paints, quilts and bakes scrumptious goodies in one of her two brick ovens, "which still keep salt dry!"

Whenever Tobit visits her, he scours the nearby woods in search of flint tools, like the knife he recently found, or other telltale signs of ancient civilizations. And he seldom misses an opportunity to explore the fogou, a cramped, valley floor cave over 2,000 years old.

Granny called out as he swerved onto the gravel drive. "Tobit, bring your bike around to the back. I just baked a fresh treacle tart!"

For ages Granny and others who have inhabited these lands have held three features of the promontory to be sacred – the hilltops, the valleys and the springs that wed land and sea. "The valley's magic," was another of Granny's oft-used phrases. Tobit prefers the springs and their source of water, the holy wells. There are over 200 holy wells in Cornwall, one for nearly every Cornish saint. Tobit, for a 15-year-old, enjoyed a precocious love of history and archaeology.

"Hi, Granny, where's *my* pie?" asked Tobit, more typical of his age, as he bounded through the door. "I am really hungry!"

"On the table, sweetie. Tobes, there's a right handsome gentleman working in the valley. If you see him, extend an invite for afternoon tea, and if you go to the fogou, take Toby. I've some clay dragons on the work bench that haven't dried," she said, her words scurrying up to him as he gulped down the last bite, half out the front door. Toby is Granny's prized Welsh corgi.

"Hi, I'm Tobit," he said to the gentleman Granny mentioned. He did not know he was speaking to an angel. Granny once told him: "Always show courtesy and respect, Tobit, for you never know when you may be speaking to an angel." In this instance, the angel was disguised as a herdsman and dresser of sycamore trees who called himself Amos.

Hatless, there was a brief whiff of white hair upon his head, a little more here and there softened his seasoned face. He wore a drab shirt and drabber trousers which were kept where they ought to be with several loops of blue binding twine that matched the colour of his affectionate eyes.

"I'm Amos, pleased to meet you, Tobit." They shook hands and made small talk before Amos came to the point. "Your grandmother mentioned that you are interested in archaeology."

"Yes, sir! In fact, there's an Iron Age fogou right over there. I'll show you, if you like," he politely offered, leading the way.

A fogou, which means simply 'cave' in Cornish, is a narrow man-made tunnel extending 30 feet or more into the earth. Large granite stones form both the roof and walls. About halfway in, and off to one side, is a chamber about large enough for one person. It's called the 'creep' and deepens the fogou's mystery.

"Archaeologists don't know what purpose fogous served," explained Tobit.

There's a sky full of theories, however. Some experts believe they were constructed for food storage, while others think they may have been intended for refuge should nearby villages come under attack, and still others relentlessly argue for religious or ritualistic usages.

"I know of one ancient practice," said Amos. "Would you like a brief demonstration?"

Tobit was keen on the idea and listened closely as Amos prepared him. He first told Tobit about the various religious cults which flourished during a spiritual renaissance throughout *Pax Romana* around the time of the birth of Christ.

In the 'Southern Lands', as Amos termed the Mediterranean rim, the cults of Diana, the Roman moon goddess, and Artemis, her Greek counterpart, along with the Egyptian goddess, Isis, were the most popular.

Amos spoke also of a Jewish mystery sect in the Holy Land called the Essenes who practised an early form of eastern religious monasticism, leading simple austere lives in preparation for the coming of the Messiah. John the Baptist was one.

In the 'Northern Lands', Celtic Ireland, Wales, Scotland, Brittany and Cornwall, Amos said the Celts were listening closely to the vates, a branch of their Druidic priesthood gifted with the power of prophecy and who at that time in history, like their southern counterparts, were proclaiming the dawn of a glorious new era.

A cornerstone of the Celtic religion of Druidism is belief in the universal cycle of birth, death and rebirth which applies not only to man but to all of creation, including civilizations and their religions. The Druids would have had to prepare their people for these monumental, but not necessarily unwelcomed, changes. Vates therefore would journey to Annwn, the Celtic Otherworld, to better understand events which might determine the survival of their culture. The fogou at Tobit's feet was used specifically for that purpose.

It was the shaman's door to the Otherworld: gateway to the gods.

Tobit entered the fogou while Toby the dog stayed with Amos. He had explored it before many times both alone and with friends. "Would this be any different?" he wondered to himself as he reached the creep and cautiously squeezed into the cumbersome, dank enclosure. "Why did Amos ask me to count to nine? That's awfully childish!"

His words slipped into darkness as he switched off his torch and settled into the creep's impersonal, silent void.

The radiation level inside this fogou, one of about a dozen in Cornwall, is 200 per cent higher than normal, and normal all around the Land's End peninsula is quite high.

"One," he whispered to himself as an unusual sense of peace and well-being cancelled his anxiety. "Two," he yawned, and quickly mumbled, "three," shaking some annoying stardust from his shoulders. "Four," was more a squirm than a word – a wriggle seeking comfort in a space designed for (sometimes uncomfortable) dreams.

Suddenly there were flashes of lightning and peals of thunder. Then Tobit beheld a beautiful girl about his own age dressed in a flowing white gown trimmed in blue. She offered him a red rose which he accepted with stunned disbelief, though in his heart he knew she was real. His eyes found hers. Tobit had never seen anyone as beautiful, a smile as enduring. She beckoned him to follow, which he did, and then she was gone. This new found world slammed shut like a door and again it seemed dark as night.

MYSTIC ROSE

Sam Bellamy growled at the knock, "It's open, Ella."

"Captain," she huffed, as she marched into his cabin. "Would you be wanting to share a few details? I've no idea who's coming on board or where we be going."

"Sorry, Ella. I was getting around to it," he said, still absorbed with his nautical charts which were thrown everywhere.

Ella is ship's cook and regardless of rank, in her own mind she keeps the *Mystic Rose* afloat. Bellamy was used to it. Indeed, her Cornish charm amused him.

He pushed his slightly rotund body away from his cherished walnut desk and plopped his black tricorn hat into place. "Let's go topside," he ordered, marching past the formidable Ella to the aft ladder. Benson was on the poop deck.

"G'day, Cap'n, another fine day indeed, sir," said Benson touching his hat. A flag lieutenant's station had to be one of the poorest commissioned assignments in any man's navy. Benson for his part was glad to be rid of it; he could act himself again. Admirals he found difficult; goddesses confounded him. "Nice uniform, sir," he teased.

Bellamy found that comment irksome. He had put a good deal of time and effort into his outfit. He donned his cocked hat atop waves of dashing dark hair. A neatly trimmed beard accented his icy blue eyes that sparkled like sea foam fizzing in summer sunshine. Around his broad chest curled a waistcoat atwitter with Celtic knots and worn over an oyster-coloured silk shirt. All told, he looked a right proper pirate captain.

"I take it the old gent's not back, Mr Benson?"

"Not yet, Cap'n. Haven't seen 'm, sir."

Bellamy pulled out his reminder details. "The boy's in the for'ard cabin. The gentleman will stay…"

"He'll be on deck looking at the stars all night, that one will, wait and see," interrupted Ella, who had taken up her favourite spot, a comfortable Barcelona abaft the mizzenmast – the mast closest to the stern. "And all my pretties are off the oak table. Dare I ask why?"

She knew why; just wanted to hear it. Bran the Blessed was coming to dinner.

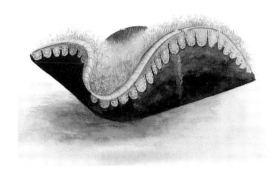

3 The Ship

Sunday, 16th July, 2000, 13.55 hours
LAMORNA COVE

"Tobit, Tobit."

Tobit recognised Amos' voice. Was he still in the fogou? Amos called again, and caught the attention of his bewildered young protégé. Tobit for his part was desperately trying to sort it out.

Medical science recently was afforded a unique opportunity to observe and study the human body whilst in a state of ecstasy. Visionaries in Bosnia claiming apparitions of Mary were scrutinised by Vatican scientists in the 1980s. They discovered that the seers, when in their daily ecstasies, were oblivious to their surroundings – even to a pin prick. The phenomenon of spiritual ecstasy is acknowledged by the scientific community and yet it eludes rational explanation for obvious reasons.

Tobit's rational mind was having no difficulty sorting the obvious: Amos stood ten feet away on the beach beside a small dinghy. Looking around, Tobit saw a hillside carpet of red campion and ox-eye daisies in late bloom among familiar heaps of huge rocks casually tossed from the disused granite quarry above Lamorna Cove. He relaxed; he wasn't far from the fogou. A sailor standing next to Amos spoke as Tobit drew closer.

"Morning, Master Tobit, it's a mighty fine day for sailing. Mighty fine!" declared Benson preparing to shove off. "Hop aboard!"

Proper niceties were handled by Amos, undaunted by the twofold task of having to invite Tobit along on a 36-hour voyage to the Celtic Otherworld, and explaining what had just happened. To put the lad at ease Amos assured Tobit that he would return to the fogou at *exactly* the minute he departed it. In other words, Tobit was now outside time and space as we know it. It wasn't difficult, Tobit was thrilled to come along.

THE SHIP · 13

Departing Lamorna Cove, Tobit admired Mermaid's Rock jutting from the ragged cliffs forming Cornwall's magnificently chiselled coastline. Then *she* appeared hove-to, wallowing in a gentle breeze. The *Mystic Rose* was the strangest sailing ship Tobit had ever seen! She was a visual smorgasbord with an outright coquettish attitude. His wide, wandering eyes riveted to the ship's prow.

"Who . . . what is that?" he exclaimed, staring at perhaps the strangest figurehead ever put to sea.

Tobit's gaze feasted on a larger than life carving of a man, not the usual half-naked nymph preferred by many a superstitious captain hoping to boost his crew's morale; perhaps their stamina too. This figurehead sported a flowing black robe and squared his arms at the elbows; palms raised as if to calm raging waters. Upon his chest puffed a large 'Z' gilded in the same brilliant goldleaf that decorated the *Rose* from stem to stern. Upon its shoulders perched two carved eagles: one with wings at rest, the other with wings spread wide, ready to soar upon jets of salty air.

"Oh, that's the great prophet Ezekiel, the father of Judaism," said Amos, momentarily absorbed in his own thoughts. "Like all nautical figureheads, he represents the spirit of the ship."

Ezekiel, prophet of the Babylonian exile

Two of the *Rose*'s flags then caught Tobit's eye. The black one with a white cross was the flag of Celtic Cornwall. It flew atop the main-mast. The other seemed intimidating and made him uneasy. Also black featuring a red hourglass in the centre, it was Sam Bellamy's personal Jolly Roger and streamed from atop the mizzen.

Pirates' flags are intended to intimidate. The bottom half of the hour glass held two-thirds of the blood-coloured shifting sand and seemed to shout: "Your time has come!" A few centuries ago this ominous flag may have been quite useful to a shipload of pirates who seldom had to open fire to take their prize. The unlucky captain of a merchant vessel coming across pirates would barter for his own life and the lives of his crew and live to sail again.

The *Mystic Rose* had no mandate to attack other vessels, or any-thing else for that matter. She is, after all, invisible; another friendly Celtic phantom ship with a captain who is, and always was, a bit over the top. According to Otherworld rules, the *Rose* could become visible if need be, and could even travel over land, but could not take prizes. Bellamy was clear on those points. So was Tobit – Amos saw to that, and assured him that there were no real pirates aboard.

Tobit watched Benson expertly guide the dinghy alongside the medieval square-rigged caravel. Bellamy would greet him at tea time, leaving his orientation to Ella. At midnight the captain would pilot the *Rose* perilously close to Samson in the Scilly Isles where others would board beneath a cloak of darkness. With Tobit and Amos safely aboard, Bellamy set sail.

4 Peculiar Time

Amos first showed Tobit his cabin then escorted him aft where Ella's welcome included milk and pie served in her cramped galley. Ella, who loved the sea almost as much as she loved her food, reminded Tobit of Granny and he quickly relaxed.

But he was full of questions such as where were they going and why, and he was unsure about what time it was. Ella pointed to the clock. It was just after three in the afternoon.

Amos noticed Tobit's quizzical expression. "You'll be on board for what will seem like 36 hours, Tobit. Our mission clocks are set to *peculiar* time, which began at 1.55 pm – the time you left the fogou. Out there in the Otherworld, time is what we make of it. For instance, we are going *back* through time right now. At midnight tonight we will have journeyed all the way back to AD 542, and at midnight tomorrow we'll have gone back even further, to AD 473. It will become clear as we sail along. You run along now with Ella."

"Let's begin up front near the fo'c's'le," suggested Ella, taking her cue and using the nautical pronunciation of forecastle. "This here's our Quiet Cabin, kind of a chapel – drop in any time. Over there's a statue of Brigid. If you don't know about her, there's books in the library next hatch up. It's worth a visit!"

That was an understatement, the *Rose*'s library was exceptional. It contained not only books about Brigid, the Celtic goddess and Christian saint, known also as St Bride, but volumes on the philosophy of history by Spengler, Toynbee, Coon and Dumezil. There were works on metaphysics, spirituality and mysticism; books on the old stones of Land's End (where Tobit lives), referring to the numerous extant megalithic monuments scattered around the Cornish peninsula.

Brigid, the Celts' favourite goddess

"What's that large bowl?" asked Tobit, still in the Quiet Cabin. The bowl, or cauldron, rested on a white marble top table in the centre of the cabin.

"It's special! That's Brigid's Cauldron of Inspiration which we are allowed to keep on the *Rose*. Brigid is the patroness of poets and prophets and mistress of inspiration. She's also the Goddess of Teinne, which we call 'Celtic Fire'. It's sacred, and tonight we'll light her cauldron with the ancient flame, to be provided by Bran the Blessed, or so I'm told. Let's move along now.

"You'll find that Amos has anticipated all your needs, so have a look round your cabin. Tea's taken at four in the galley. It's a small ship, Tobit, so muck right in, we're delighted to have you," she said, waving good-bye over her shoulder as she hastened down the companionway.

Benson tapped on Tobit's cabin door at half three. "Cap'n'd like to welcome you aboard. I'll show you topside," he said to a drowsy Tobit who had dozed in his homey bunk.

Bellamy waited on his quarter deck and Benson touched his hat as they approached. "Welcome aboard the *Mystic Rose*, Tobit. Let's disperse with formalities, call me either Sam or Captain, whichever you prefer."

"Yes, sir," said Tobit, immediately disregarding his instructions and bringing a smile to Bellamy's naturally appealing face. "Thank you for…" he chased the proper expression, "inviting me."

"Come over here lad and allow me to show you something," continued Bellamy, escorting Tobit to the starboard rail. The view was breathtaking! The *Rose* was crossing $5°42'$ West Longitude along the fiftieth parallel two miles off the western tip of Britain where the St George's, Bristol, and English Channels infiltrate the Celtic Sea. Tobit admired the spectacular rocky coastline of the peninsula, its cliffs and coves, and could see as far north as Land's End itself.

"That's Carn Lês Boel, the exact spot where the line of the Midsummer sunrise completes its course across the island," said Bellamy.

Tobit had heard of the 'Dragon Line'. It traces a path from the East Anglian coast through Wessex and into the north Atlantic (or the Celtic Sea) at Carn Lês Boel. The line is usually associated with St Michael's Mount near Penzance, although on the western side of

Mount's Bay it crosses Tobit's village of St Buryan. In fact, St Buryan Church sits right upon the line, as does the famous Tor at Glastonbury with its small chapel dedicated to St Michael; numerous other Christian churches associated with dragon slaying saints; and the famous stone circle at Avebury, the Dragon Line's most familiar, most sacred site from prehistory.

"Tomorrow night, Tobit, we'll be sailing on another of these 'mystical energy' lines as we make for an inlet in north Cornwall named Bossiney Haven and perhaps we'll even catch a glimpse of the druid priest it was named after. The sea may get a little rough, it always does when we sail into the seam of time, but we'll need you topside for the fireworks all the same. So remember, sleep-in tomorrow morning, and don't eat after six tomorrow evening. Don't want you getting sea sick, do we?"

'Sea sick' worried Tobit even more than 'fireworks'. Furthermore, he still didn't appreciate why Sam was dressed up as a pirate. "Is it dangerous?" he asked in a small voice.

"Not at all, lad! It's just that whenever the *Rose* sails into two time dimensions simultaneously…" Now the captain was chasing proper expressions. "Tomorrow night we'll peek into the present, acquiring both the 6th and the 21st centuries concurrently – at the same time, so to speak." He gave up the useless chase. "Whenever it happens we kick up a little dust, that's all. Don't worry about it, it's tea time! C'mon," he muttered, annoyed with his deficiency in matters temporal. "C'mon!"

5 *The Video*

Ella's afternoon tea was always picture postcard perfect and offered something for everyone. Of course, there was the traditional Cornish cream tea featuring freshly baked scones, homemade strawberry jam and the *pièce de résistance*, Cornish clotted cream.

The recipe for clotted cream was imported to Cornwall before Christianity by descendants of Phoenician traders who bartered Tyrian purple cloth, exquisite Greek olives and oil, and Mediterranean wine at continental ports before sailing on to trade for Cornish tin and copper. Their ships docked at a tiny island called 'Iktis' which could be reached by land at low water over 2,000 years ago, just as it can today. Iktis is now called St Michael's Mount.

Ella had no need of Phoenician recipes. She made her own clotted cream, which was exceptional. "Jersey milk's the best," she frequently exclaimed. "Got to have that high butterfat for good clotted cream. Gives it the golden crust!" In addition to scones, she served her delicious little finger sandwiches first popularised during the reign of King Edward VII, Duke of Cornwall.

Everyone gathered for the tea ceremony around the oak table and began smothering their scones – jam before cream, the proper Cornish way. Ella kept an alert eye for transgressors. She surveyed the table; the pre-occupied mouths. "Let's tell Tobit about Bran the Blessed, Captain."

"Here we go!" he gulped, accidentally poking his nose in his scone and meeting the fate feared in Devonshire, where jam's on top. "When is it, Benson?" he asked.

Benson checked his chronometer. "Passing through AD 600, sir."

"Right. The funeral ferryboat will leave the cove soon, which means the procession should commence within the hour," guessed the captain.

None of this temporising made any sense at all to Tobit. Bellamy,

THE VIDEO · 19

having demonstrated another deficiency – with a scone, no less –
looked around the table for a rescuer. He was not going to be spurred
into a discussion about Bran, Ella's least favourite man-god.

"Tobit, Bran travels with a very special bird and both are boarding
tonight at midnight. Perhaps the video would be helpful, Captain,"
suggested Amos.

Ella, not to be denied, came straight out with it: "Birds of a feather
is more like it! Bran's an obnoxious talking head travelling with a
crow. More tea, Captain?"

"No thank you, Ella. What say we all adjourn to the media room
and watch the video as Amos suggested," said Bellamy. "That should
help Tobit, as well as re-acquaint the rest of us with the history
behind our mission."

Everyone settled into the cramped area dubbed the media room.
"This is the latest in bardic technology, so to speak," boasted the captain. "Roll, please."

The narrator, a pleasant middle-aged man with a gravelly voice,
began:

"Today, in the Year of Our Lord 542 in the holy land of Belerion, is
a day tarnished by tragedy. Mortally wounded in combat and slowly
departing this dimension is one of the great military leaders of his day;
a man known by many for his chivalry, integrity and charm; a great
warrior who served his countrymen unselfishly with dedication, tenac-
ity and skill at arms. It is a day like all days, except you are there!"

Field correspondent: "With us is Morgan le Fay who is attending the
commander. Tell us, Miss le Fay, what are his chances?"

"Not good, I fear. Not good at all. You do understand, don't you,
that he must die? He has fought the good fight and his work is finished.
He has achieved the victory and will accept his destiny. I will see to him
now, if you will excuse me. You should speak to the holy woman. Look,
she goes there!"

"Madam! Madam, please. May we have a word?"

"Why, yes, of course. It is both a sad and a joyful day, is it not? I
have come to bless him and to send him on his journey. Miss le Fay
and her sisters will deliver him to the gods. I bless them all, you know,

Belerion – an
ancient name for
Land's End

the dead, the dying. That is why they are brought to my humble oratory."

"This ritual: Is it Christian?"

"Celtic Christian, Milord! He was a devout Christian warrior who defeated the heathen Saxons. He won many front-line battles. He secured the peace and now it remains for us and the truths we cherish to take root in this rocky soil. We are the remnant flock, Milord."

"May I ask your name, madam?"

"They call me the holy woman of the burying place. There were many before me and others shall surely follow. Perhaps I will take the name 'Buriana', as I am known by my sisters. Here in my little oratory we tend the sacred flame, an ancient tradition. I must go, but one of his followers is there, on the left. Speak with him, he hails from this area."

"Sir, my condolences, I am told you were one of his followers."

"Thank you. Yes, I am Sir Perceval of Trevorgans, grandson of King Gereint. I served with him from the beginning. He was a great leader whom we shall miss. We, his friends, will escort his body to the ferryman for his voyage to Avalon. There it is said that he shall receive a king's burial. I have my doubts, however. The healing women who tend him – they are magicians, you know, like the great Merlyn. I must bid you adieu, sire. Sir Bedivere requires my counsel."

"Miss le Fay, excuse me again please, just one final question, if I may? One of the knights, a Sir Perceval, has raised questions about the burial on Avalon. Could you possibly clear that up for us?"

"May the gods give me patience! Come over here where no one may overhear. We will take his body through the woods to the holy well. Later at the cove it will appear to the mourners that he is moribund as you see him now, but it will not be so. The crone waits at her holy well and will transform his soul into a chough, a raven with red feet and a curved red beak, common in our land. As we depart on the ferry, the bird will be among us."

"This old woman, this crone, I beg leave to speak with her! Where may I find her, please?"

"Sir, you don't understand. She is Brigid, daughter of the Dagda, the Lady of the Lake, the Woman Clothed with the Sun. The moon and stars lie at her feet. She does not grant interviews!"

"And the slain warrior, how is he called?"

"Surely, you mock me, sir. Why, he is King Arthur – *Rex quondam, rexque futurus* – our once and future king!"

The narrator: "Tobit has just witnessed what happened in his neighbourhood some fourteen hundred and fifty years ago.

"Buriana became Saint Buriana, literally 'the holy woman of Buryan', the burying place, known simply as 'the sacred hill' to the ancients. Today a church stands on the ground of her oratory, sharing its name with the village which grew around it, St Buryan.

"And that's the way it was – a day like everyday filled with joy and sorrow, except you were there. From all of us in the Celtic Otherworld, goodnight."

"Wow!" said Tobit. He turned to find the darkened theatre empty. He raced topside. No one. The galley, library, chapel; all empty.

Buriana

6 The Piskies

Music and sounds of distant merrymaking accentuated the constant creaking of the rigging, the splish-splash of the ocean slapping against the *Rose*'s bow, the groaning of the oak timbers as Tobit, looking to find a familiar face, felt his way inch by inch into an unfamiliar area of the ship.

A hatch squeaked open. Barely having had time to gather his wits, Tobit froze like ice as he felt a tug on his trouser leg. Goose bumps raced down his arms.

"Mr Pem-David! Turn him loose! Mind your manners. Sorry, Tobit, he's simply fascinated by mortals," declared the captain looking around. "Tobit, this is Mr Pem-David, call him 'Pem', he's one of my company of Little Green People from the Isle of Gwales."

Tobit had never heard of it; didn't really believe in little green people. "Pleased to meet you," said Tobit, remembering his manners and reaching to shake his hand. Pem grabbed Tobit's leg instead and hugged it again.

"Let's go inside," said Bellamy, embarrassed by his boatswain's antics.

There was a party going on in the dayroom. "They always party when the moon is full, come hell or high water, so to speak," joked Bellamy.

There were two dozen of them. All looked as if they were three feet tall, give or take an inch or two, and wore green from head to toe except Pem, whose pointy hood was red, owing to his warrant. They hoisted tankards in salutation as Tobit occasionally caught the odd shy eye. And they all seemed to be drinking milk.

"Have some, Tobit," Ella said from behind, not intending to startle him. "Jersey milk – fresh, too! Bet you've never been to a piskie party?"

She was correct, of course. In fact, few mortals have seen a piskie.

They're faeries who serve as the spirits of nature. These particular sea-piskies attend the children of Llyr, gods of the Otherworld, and would sup this festive night with their hero, Bran the Blessed, King of Britain, and be regaled once again with his enchanting tales of triumph and glory.

Pem gave Tobit's leg another friendly hug and jumped onto a nearby table. He clapped his hands to a two-four beat whilst tacking on some light soft-shoe. It was all the encouragement needed; the assembly broke into song.

> *"Dance, then, wherever you may be;*
> *I am the Lord of the Dance, said he,*
> *and I'll lead you all, wherever you may be,*
> *and I'll lead you all in the dance, said he."*

Pem intoned the first verse:

> *"I danced in the morning*
> *when the world was begun,*
> *and I danced in the moon*
> *and the stars and the sun,*
> *and I came down from heaven*
> *and I danced on the earth;*
> *at Bethlehem*
> *I had my birth."*

SYDNEY CARTER

"Sorry to desert you, Tobit," apologised Amos over the chorus. "I suppose everyone else left thinking I was still in the theatre."

"Was that really King Arthur in the video?"

"Let's go topside, shall we, this celebration may go on until midnight."

The night time sky glided over the few remaining whiffs of pink and grey clouds resting on the horizon as the *Rose* sailed westward toward the Scilly Isles. Amos showed Tobit to the poop deck.

"Look at the sky, Tobit, and tell me what you see."

"Well, that's the Plough. And that's the north star," said Tobit, proudly pointing to the cluster of over 100 stars which includes

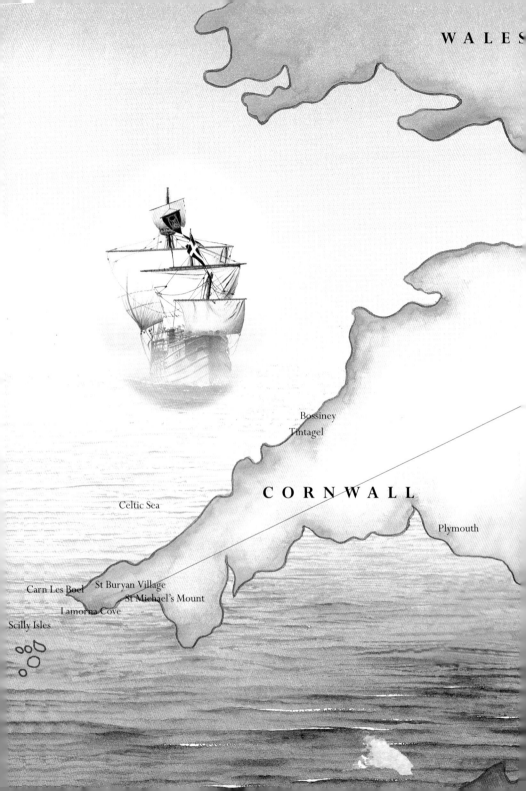

WALES

Bossiney
Tintagel

CORNWALL

Celtic Sea

Plymouth

Carn Les Boel   St Buryan Village
                 St Michael's Mount
       Lamorna Cove
Scilly Isles

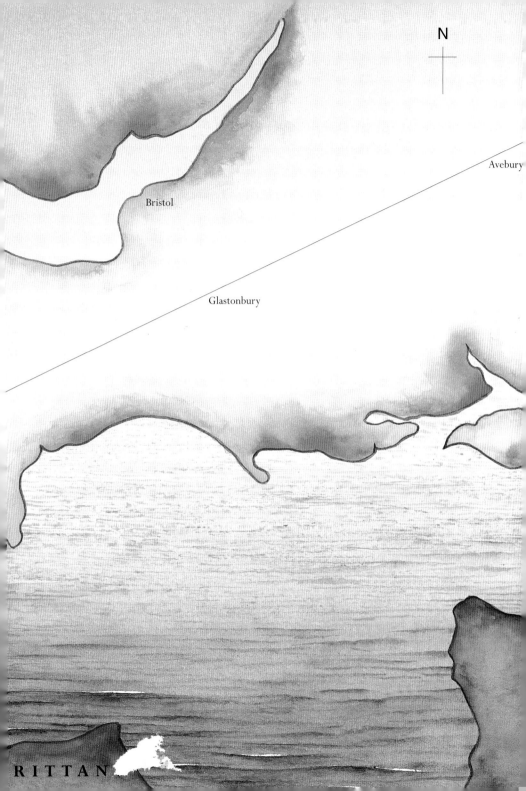

N

Avebury

Bristol

Glastonbury

RITTAN

Ursa Major, called the 'Plough' or the 'Big Dipper', and Ursa Minor, the constellation home of Polaris, our north polar star.

"Excellent! And the bright star over there – do you know it?" Amos continued after a brief pause. "That's Arcturus in the constellation Boötes, or the Herdsman. It's the second brightest star in the northern sky. Now what's the first?"

"The sun," replied Tobit, without pausing.

"Almost had you!" laughed Amos. "See that tight 'W' shaped cluster? That's Cassiopeia and that's Draco, the Dragon. In ancient times around 2500 BC when the pyramids were being built in the south and the stone circles in the north, one of its stars was the pole star."

"There's more than one North Star?"

"It's known as the 'precession of the equinoxes'. The great cycle takes 25,800 years and involves five different stars which in turn act as our north star.

"King Arthur is named after Ursa Minor, The Little Bear, that appeared to push Draco, The Dragon, off his northern throne long ago. In the ancient tongue 'little bear' is pronounced 'arth-vawr' or 'Arthur' – so the famous King has been around for a while. He was like a *god-saviour* to the northern people and manifests himself in their history in times of greatest need."

"There's *more* than one God!?"

"Well, there is Yahweh, God of the Jews; Jesus, God of the Christians, and Allah, God of the Muslims. Here's my point, Tobit: those are all categories. God is Ultimate Mystery – beyond man's concepts and ideas. Mankind has lost its sense of *mystery*. Arthur represents such *mystery* – he's found in myth and folklore all over Europe."

"So, he's not real then."

"Oh, sure he is! He's a *spiritual reality*."

7 Bran the Blessed

AD 542
THE SCILLY ISLES

The *Rose* anchored off the coast of Samson Island as midnight drew near. Bellamy, in his quarters, heard rustling footsteps overhead.

"Ahoy, ahoy," called the ferryman. "I have your car . . . your passengers."

Benson reached for the sack which weighed some 30 pounds and, to no one's surprise, its contents launched into a harangue. "Careful! Will you. We don't fancy being bumped about. We're not cargo, regardless what this fool calls us. Will not someone disburden us of this oppressive confinement!" he demanded.

"Take the sack below, Mr Benson," said Bellamy arriving on the scene and immediately inclining his attention toward the attractive lady in the dory. "Good evening Miss le Fay. Will you and Mr Barin care to join us for dinner?"

"Most kind of you, Captain, perhaps another time."

"No time like the present, so to speak."

"Okay. You two cut it out," said Barin, unamused by witticisms about time; less with Bellamy's goofy coquetry. "Safe passage to you, sir."

The captain touched his hat and forced a smile to shine through his disappointment. He turned away and missed seeing Miss le Fay's affectionate wave as the dory drifted into the night, a wave observed by two darting eyes from atop the mizzenmast.

The head of Bran the Blessed, no longer oppressed or confined, had been placed in the centre of the oak table to await protocol.

"Welcome, everyone," Bellamy began. "We look forward to an exciting day aboard the *Mystic Rose*. Shortly we will sail for Bossiney in the parish of Tintagel and arrive in the area around AD 475. When is it now, Mr Benson?"

"Time's anchored at AD 542, sir."

"Oh, right! We have an exciting manoeuvre planned, an 'in-time' replay from AD 473 conjoined hard and fast to a 'real-time' event today, 16 July, 2000, in the year of the dragon. Our new friend, Tobit, makes this possible." The group delighted Tobit with a polite round of applause.

"You are all, of course, expected topside to witness the moment. Don't forget to wear waterproofs as it gets rather wet when we rip the stitches, so to speak. Now it is my honour to present Bran ab Llyr known to all as Bran the Blessed, King of Britain, Otherworld custodian of the Pendragon Cauldron of Rebirth."

His head was enormous — twice and half again the size of an average human head. He had enormous red hair and an enormous red beard. But you first noticed his eyes. The pupils themselves exceeded the size of an average human eye and were wreathed by verdant green irises. They circled the room and landed on Tobit who sat cross-legged between Amos and Pem-David.

"Watch this, lad!" he said, after the applause and chanting quieted.

Immediately his enormous head sprouted antlers like a grand stag. They grew larger and larger, shaping into proportion as Pem and the piskies jumped up and down and clapped their hands with joy. "Bran! Bran! Bran…" they chanted louder than before.

He wasn't done. "I am the god who sets the head on fire!" he stoutly proclaimed. Immediately the antlers' eight points burst into flame and the piskies roared their approval.

"How 'bout that, lad?" he asked Tobit, who realised no answer was expected. "Thank you, Captain, for your warm presentation. We look forward with all those present, to this victorious day. Please, everyone, be seated. Begin your feast!"

Turning his eyes again to Tobit he asked in a gentler tone, "What do you know of us, lad? You may refer to us as, 'Your Majesty'."

"Very little, Your Majesty."

He winced, then allowed his awesome presence to engage everyone's full attention.

"When the world was young, the gods named us to defend the sovereignty of this green and pleasant land, which has become, to both our surprise and delight, a great nation. In doing so, we lifted armies upon our back and our shoulders held high the noblest heroes of battles won and lost. In the final conflict of the Great Irish War we were most unfortunately wounded in our royal foot by a poisoned spear – a wound which would have proved to be fatal had we not acted decisively.

"Knowing time was short, we commanded Prince Dyfed, one of our seven surviving compatriots, to sever our royal head and bury it where the Tower of London now stands. From there we could face the Channel and repel the enemy. We might add that the Channel was our idea, and a very good one. Still is!"

"Tell us about the Assembly of the Wondrous Head," one of the piskies shouted impatiently.

"Yes, yes, in due time. But rather than allow us to be buried, the gods dispatched royal ravens in our stead to Londinium and they have loyally remained there ever since. We then were carried to our castle at Gwales where we entertained friends and presided over great feasts at the Assembly.

"One fateful day, the gods opened the forbidden window which overlooked Cornwall, and reality poured through. It was the sign we awaited!

"We released the two dragons buried by the treacherous Vortigern and Arthur was born. It was in the Year of Our Lord, 473."

"That was then, this is now, more or less," added the captain.

"*Essato!*" responded Bran. "It is our royal understanding that Vortigern's daughter, Saint someone or the other, will join us. This is most fitting, dear friends: the irony of the gods."

Ella had heard enough. "Saint Materiana, you mead-guzzling, chauvinistic relic of a headhunter. Her name is Saint Materiana!"

"Of course it is. And how are you, our littlest angel?"

"Don't be startin' with me, Branny Boy! Yer'll be findin' 'erself locked in 'ere with me big cat, yer will." Ella's Cornish accent was a reliable gauge of how annoyed she was.

"There's a *cat* on board?" Bran looked worried.

"We'll keep him out of your hair," said Bellamy, playing along – there was no cat. "With permission, Your Majesty, my officers and I will take our leave, but carry on. Breakfast is served when the watch is called. See you then."

"Regretfully, Tobit and I must also depart," declared Amos seizing an inoffensive opportunity to leave. "It has been... *enlightening*."

AD 473
BOSSINEY, NORTH CORNWALL

One more day; a full day's work to go. Cini finished this day exhausted and stole a moment to relax and admire the sea view from his favourite nook above the haven. The chief priest of the Dumnonii tribe, the Celts of south-western Britannia, as the Romans called it, ticked through the checklist in his mind's eye once more.

Bossiney – Celtic name meaning 'Cini's place'

Every day for the past week the men from his village had laboured hard gathering sticks and logs and carrying them from the glens and forests up the hill to the barrow. Tomorrow Cini would inspect the result – a huge pile of timber which when kindled would become the largest bonfire his people had ever witnessed. Two other fires (there would be three altogether) would prove to be more difficult and he prayed that the brave boys who had volunteered for the dangerous mission would gain the gods' protection.

He could put it off no longer; that last item on his list which made him jumpy whenever it crossed his mind. He must explain, or at least try to explain, to the King of Cornwall, that neither he nor any of the elders would be permitted by the gods to witness tomorrow night's secret ritual. Later he would put the list out of his mind and sleep.

8 The Symbols

Bellamy relished those private moments he stole at the end of each day when he retreated to his 'sacred place' to relax, read and reflect. He often reflected upon fate. For example, he and Benson might have chosen any ship from the list the admiral-goddess handed him that day two months ago and renamed it *Mystic Rose*.

It was necessary, however, to fulfil several criteria which he knew intuitively were important. He wanted a ship built and christened in a Celtic land. He required a small vessel for this mission, one with a reputable past; a past shrouded in mystery would be even better. And he sought symbolism, the language of the gods that honed his Celtic instincts and fired his Celtic character. Benson laid out the solution.

"Wales!"

"Sorry, Mr Benson, I don't follow. If that's the name of a ship, it's not on my list."

"It's perfect, Captain, read this," Benson persisted. Benson was a good first lieutenant and Bellamy prized his initiative and enthusiasm.

> This ship, a fifteenth-century caravel, was built in Bristol and led an expedition in 1498 commissioned by Henry Tudor, Henry VII of England, a Welshman. The ship, her captain, Giovanni Caboto, an Italian navigator, and four other vessels had mysteriously vanished into the dark depths of maritime martyrdom.

"Excellent work, Mr Benson! A good find, indeed." But what appealed most to Bellamy in Benson's report was its symbolism and symmetry.

The history was certainly intriguing.

> Victorious in the battle of Bosworth, Henry claimed the British crown in Wales under the banner of the Red Dragon. Henry Tudor frequently boasted that *he* restored the *true* royal line to the British throne after the Saxon and Norman usurpers. His first son, born in 1486, was christened Arthur, and Henry believed that the Tudors of Wales were in fact descended from King Arthur, although his son never became Arthur II as he planned.

Giovanni Caboto's second ship disappeared

"Proper job," he told Benson. "Let's check her availability."

No surprise there! Giovanni Caboto's old ship topped the list and would be named *Mystic Rose*. There was a footnote on Benson's report:

> In 1497 Giovanni Caboto charted the North Atlantic route leading to the New World

– Bellamy's route two centuries later when he sailed for New Plymouth.

A medieval caravel was a small, square-rigged, three masted vessel. In those days, square rigging helped calm a seaman's worst fears: light, failing winds that disrupted steerageway, potentially exposing an unmanoeuvrable ship to scheming currents swirling off rock infested coastlines. The infestation was especially bad where the *Rose* was destined. Lye Rock near Bossiney claimed the Italian *Iota* in 1893 and the cabin boy, who was on his maiden voyage, perished. The youth was buried at nearby Tintagel in the parish churchyard of St Materiana.

To improve manoeuvrability the caravel was typically built short and nicely rounded, and was designed to raise over 2,500 square feet of canvas; to pitch and roll in a vicious storm without making water.

Bellamy had the ideal ship. A ship he could sail into Bossiney Haven, complete his mission, and eluding Lye Rock, box-haul to the relative safety of open sea. In excellent conditions this difficult feat of navigation required great skill. Bellamy would have to perform it at night in gale force winds and in seas confused by an Otherworld ship ripping across the field of time. His destiny would greet its moment of truth.

As time nears
BOSSINEY

Low water. Cini's boys positioned a huge cauldron as close to the edge of Lye Rock as possible, much to the displeasure of the resident puffin colony forced to flee falling stones. Whale oil – gallons of it, followed. Across the inlet similar activity was taking place.

Even at low tide those boys were barely able to access Saddle Rocks on foot from the headland. Up its slippery spine they crawled. Down came the ropes, tossed to the men waiting below in tiny fishing boats. Up went two smaller cauldrons which were positioned one next to the other on the rock's highest point. Ropes were tossed down again to fetch the oil in large goatskin bags.

The plan was simple, really. Upon receiving the signal, nine men using nine sticks taken from nine different types of wood would light the sacred bonfire atop Condolen Hill. Sacred fires were always lit ceremoniously in an elaborate manner. This one would be visible for miles. Eight runners chosen from among the tribe's most pious women would scamper down the hillside carrying torches to archers stationed around the inlet, their arrows tipped with oil soaked reed.

The ninth runner, a priest, would take his torch through the glen to the holy well to light a different ritual.

From bonfire to cauldrons, the lighting would take three parts of an hour, leaving ample time before midnight for all participants including the priests to return to their huts. Cini would remain on the meadow overlooking the haven. From there he would have a good view of the ship, as well as of the frail old man standing across the gorge.

9 *The Mission*

"Call all hands, Mr Pem-David." The chirping of the bosun's pipes brought everyone scrambling to the poop deck, Bellamy's favourite gathering place. One piskie arrived carrying the head of Bran the Blessed on a short spar.

"Tonight we throw caution to the wind, so to speak. In a few hours we will anchor several miles at sea north-west of Bossiney and allow time to catch up to us. At dark we will sail into Bossiney Haven. Eleven-ish we will see several beacons ashore. Also at that hour the *Rose* will kick up a storm as we breech the 21st century. We go in on the ninth wave from midnight. When is it now, Mr Benson?"

"AD 512, sir."

"Right. Not far. At 13.55 hours we'll acquire AD 495 and Bran the Blessed will have a few words of inspiration for us."

The captain then briefed everyone on the technical aspects of the manoeuvre. Winds gusting to force 8 gale and shifting direction twice were expected. With the first shift they would heave-to. That would drop them like a rock off the ninth wave's back before it crashed into the cliffs. A gibe with the second shift would enable them to avoid the terror of Lye Rock and sail over the diminishing swells into open sea.

Amos felt Tobit's anxiety and offered some words of encouragement. "Don't be afraid tonight, Tobit. The storm may rattle your nerves but we are perfectly safe aboard this ship. Under ordinary circumstances you could spend your entire life aboard the *Rose* and never have to touch the tiller. Wind and sea obey her.

"Remember these words, Tobit, and fear not. Tonight we herald the dawn of a spiritual renaissance, a new era in the story of man. The seeds we sow upon the land will grow of their own accord; you and your generation shall be first fruits of the harvest."

13.55 Hours, peculiar

Another summer day yawned and stretched in afternoon sunshine. "Ambrosius is dead," announced Bran to the muster on the poop deck. "The accession of the Pendragon Clan therefore is accomplished. However, our task lies before us as we travel through another 22 years of history. The Great King Arthur, you all know, defeats the Saxons at Mount Badon thus ensuring a remnant flock to inform the spiritual future of mankind – a Celtic remnant. From this remnant the gods have chosen young Tobit of Saint Buryan to stand on the bow of tomorrow, to seal the eternal destiny of the Celtic people – the return of the Pendragon! The moon is full and in eclipse in the southern lands. How say you, lad?"

King Arthur defeats the Saxons, halting their westward advance for 50 years

Tobit felt the sting of a zillion invisible spirits. "I accept! Your Majesty," he said proudly. Amos had prepared him well for this moment.

"*Bravo!*" exclaimed Bran.

"Here, here!" shouted the piskies.

"Deck, there, sail ho! Off the port bow, sir!"

Bellamy snapped open his glass. "Looks like a small craft with three aboard. Bring the ship to, if you please, Mr Benson."

"Aye aye, sir."

Bellamy was not surprised. The seaways between Cornwall's northern coast, Ireland and Wales were quite busy in the late 5th and early 6th centuries with hermits leaving convents and monasteries for Cornwall not, as popular legend has it, to convert the heathens – Cornwall had been converted for centuries – but rather on lifelong pilgrimage. For Celtic Christians, it was a form of martyrdom to leave home for a strange land and the glory of Christ. The Spirit led them to Cornwall, the 'Land of Promise'.

"Who are they?" asked Pem-David.

"Two nuns and a monk," replied Amos. "Sisters Breaca and Crowan and a wanderer named Germoe. They have connections to a foundation in Kildare and carry the Sacred Flame of Saint Brigid, the Christianised Brigid, Goddess of the Land."

They never saw the *Rose*. She was far, far away at a misty intersection in time.

10 The Colours

Tobit, apprehensive and hungry, walked into Ella's galley. "Delighted you stopped in. How 'bout some milk and shortbread?"

"I'm not very hungry."

"Nervous about being alone up there on the fo'c's'le tonight?"

"A little," fibbed Tobit again.

"It's natural. Here's some milk and shortbread anyway. Don't worry about what the captain said. You have to eat something and you've had nothing since tea." Tobit dug in. "But 'tis no cause to worry, Tobit. When the gods inspire a task, they grant the grace to accomplish it. The chough that boarded with Bran must begin its short flight tonight from your strong shoulder. It's one of the rules."

"Why?"

"Who knows? It's baffled us for ages! But God wrote the rules and is faithful to them."

"Is Sam dressed like a pirate because it's one of the rules, too."

"No. It's not important. You have to wear something."

"Why must we sail so close to the cliffs?"

"Well, I recall reading that crows become disorientated over water. But the real reason is the symbolism of the ninth wave. You can read about that in the library, but finish your milk first." She pushed the glass toward Tobit and gave him a warm, angelic smile.

The library was quiet, both watches were busy topside. Tobit found a book on Celtic mythology and began reading. When Amos came in, he closed it.

"Amos, what's the symbolism of the ninth wave?"

"There are two important aspects to it. The number 'nine' is significant in many mythologies. It's the sacred three times three. The ninth wave is symbolic because it marks the sovereignty of the coastline. Beyond the ninth wave denotes exile. When the *Rose* sails in on the ninth wave tonight it's like a return from exile, a restoration symbolising spiritual intervention in human history," explained Amos.

The sharp shrill of the bosun's whistle roused everyone's attention and Tobit and Amos hurried topside.

"Hoist the colours!" ordered Pem-David.

The black and white Cornwall ensign ran up the mainmast whilst on the foremast the Welsh flag unfurled, or was it? It was white, but without the usual green bottom, and the red dragon was on a shield.

The flag of Henry VII

The third banner surprised everyone as they watched it stream open from the mizzen. It was pearly white trimmed in green with a huge green shamrock at its centre.

"What's that one?" Tobit asked Amos.

"I expect it's the personal flag of Saint Patrick. Best we get below and into our waterproofs and wellies. It's almost time."

11 The Birth

22.30 hours, peculiar
MYSTIC ROSE

The *Rose* answered the first whiffs of the evening sea breeze with creaks and groans.

"Showtime, Mr Benson," said Bellamy, touching his cocked hat as he emerged from the companion. "Aloft, there! Keep a good look-out!"

"Aye aye, sir," shouted the piskie from the top foremast yard.

The moony night unveiled bright stars as a curtain of darkness draped the horizon. Another cat's-paw of refreshing, cool leeward breeze clawed insistently at the rigging.

"Main tops'l braces!"

"Aye aye, sir."

Seemingly cued by unseen forces, an interaction of solar wind and the outer atmosphere produced a bombardment of energetic protons which flickered on and off in the northern sky. The flashing greenish-blue lights were observed by a priest at the barrow who gave the nod to nine eager men; the bonfire was minutes away.

"Deck, there! Aurora aft, sir. The sky's a light show!"

It was indeed! Usually observed only above $67°$ North Latitude in the 'aurora zone', the Northern Lights are infrequently spotted as far south as $50°$ latitude. Then another sign – Bellamy expected it! First a sizzle, then a distinct crackling of atmospheric electricity stoked all three masts with tips of faint light.

"Saint Elmo's fire!" shouted a dozen voices.

"All hands, make sail! Take a bearing, Mr Pem-David."

The sea breeze filled the mainsail and the little ship paid off toward Bossiney Haven into an odour of darkness.

"Underway, sir," announced Benson as the rudder cut into the water.

"Deck, there! Lights ashore, sir."

A distinct serpentine string of lights slivered down the hillside from the huge bonfire, clearly visible now above the starboard bow.

"One point a-starboard, Mr Benson! Steer on the beacon!"

"Steady on the beacon, sir."

Bellamy enjoyed utmost confidence in Benson's seamanship. But few men were the captain's equal when it came to coastal navigation, an essential skill for a pirate skipper used to vanishing into lairs nestled among coves and inlets where no sane pursuer would dare to follow.

"Deck, there! Two more beacons, sir. One a-starb'rd, other a-larb'rd, sir!"

The archers' aim had been true; the cauldrons were ablaze. These essential navigation aids indicated the inlet's corners and eased Bellamy's mind. He turned to Tobit who was huddled close to Ella.

"Tobit, you'll be escorted to the fo'c's'le before the first wave. Mr Pem-David will go with you, so don't be afraid. He's devised a special harness to belay you to the foremast. After we let go the ninth wave, he'll bring you back to the helm. Understood, laddy?"

"Yes, Captain."

"Very well. What of Bran, Mr Pem-David?"

"Another special rig, sir. A spar secured to the taffrail. We tested it earlier. He reluctantly approved, sir."

Bellamy noted the look of relief on Ella's face. Bran could hoot and holler from the poop deck out of sight – if not out of earshot.

"Very well. Best put him in place. We don't have long."

"Aye aye, sir."

"Wind's gone foul, sir," proclaimed the officer of the watch, a Pembrokeshire veteran from previous Otherworld voyages.

Bellamy expected that, too. The sails flapped persistently as the *Rose* yawed first one way, then the other.

"Steer small, Mr Benson."

The *Rose* lay becalmed two miles out, her final staging area, awaiting the change in the wind's direction.

The squall, or whatever it was, caused the ship to leap suddenly.

"Hands on the halyards!"

She lurched again as the wind danced around, a puff here, a puff there on the lightened canvas. Rain began falling; the sea and wind sought harmony as a heavy roller hurled sea spray over the rails then rumbled lazily toward the coast.

"Full and by, sir." The *Rose* laid over, wind off the starboard bow as the storm flexed its muscle.

They were windward now, sailing close-hauled and steady as the sea surged on both sides. The rain slackened; distant thunder rumbled out to sea; south-easterly winds whistled through the sheets as the robust inland storm east of Bossiney kicked its frenzy toward a sister low pressure trough circling astern.

The *Rose*, designed somewhat like a giant, floating bathtub, was making two knots through confused water, rolling from side to side amidst rapidly growing swells.

"Wind gusting 30 and more, sir!"

"Very well, Mr Benson," Bellamy calmly responded, appreciating the implicit suggestion. "Perhaps you should have Mr Pem-David reef the tops'l."

The beacons atop the two rock outcrops shone brighter as the *Rose* leaped effortlessly over each successive swell. Benson shot Bellamy a wry glance through the unending sea spray. "Zero-hundred hours, sir. It's when!" he quipped.

"Deck, there!" screamed the foremast lookout as if he'd seen a ghost. "A-larb'rd, sir," were the only other words he found.

"My god!" exclaimed Ella from behind.

"All right!" cried Bran the Blessed from above.

"Lo and behold! Saint Patrick!" declared Amos.

The apparition appeared suspended over the sea as a bishop with mitre and matching chasuble of emerald green taffeta embroidered with thousands of tiny Celtic crosses crafted in mother of pearl. He carried a simple shepherd's staff.

The seas hushed as he raised his right hand.

"Let us bind ourselves tonight to the holy power of the Trinity and pray that Christ be with us in the wind, which breathes destiny upon

Saint Patrick, the Celts' favourite saint

the seas, and in the waves, which undergird our hopes and our dreams. May the High King of Heaven bless you, each and all."

"Mr Pem-David, I would be pleased if you would escort young Tobit to the fo'c's'le," said Bellamy.

"Aye aye, sir. Straight away!"

Lightning flashed like Manannan's Sword, provoking a deafening clap of thunder as the storm reasserted its primacy. Tobit felt two hands rest firmly upon his shoulders as he took his place on the bow.

"Bear up, Mr Benson. Point high!"

That's as close to the wind as the ship can sail and manage steerageway. Suddenly she lifted as the water beneath her hull bulged; piercing wind armed with stinging rain-pellets terrorised canvas, faces, even the ocean itself, if it were possible. Higher still – on a heavy wall of water she heaved. Up, up, marching to a flashing baton, a pounding kettledrum of thunder; aching, longing for relief but resolute; determined.

The sails flapped once, twice, behind a rampaging wave that blanketed the wind. The little ship slid down its watery spine. That was the first wave, another eight will follow.

Tobit was hanging on.

"Hang on, Tobit!" shouted Pem approvingly. Tobit tried to turn around but was frozen, not with fear so much as with fascination.

Raindrops splattered the deck like globs of warm butter. Up the ladder again, higher than before. Moonlight curved around swirling clouds revealing a steep rocky coastline fighting a losing battle against an angry avalanche of water.

Everyone on deck was thoroughly soaked, waterproofs or no. Up, up, again, like a roller coaster climbing backwards, nearing, sensing the summit as its motion slowed, slowed, and then…

Wild, frightening exhilaration!

"I've lost count, Mr Benson."

"Easily forgiven," thought Benson. Rock strewn cliffs, gale force winds, a rough, billowy sea. Who's counting waves?

"That was two, Captain," pestered Ella, who was counting not only the waves, but timing the intervals between them.

Manannan – a Celtic god after whom the Isle of Man is named

Waves three, four, five, six and seven brought the ship further and further into the inlet – close enough to glimpse the storm's pent-up fury buffeting the cliffs, flooding the narrow neck of the ravine with sudsy saltwater, and swamping the delicate brook tumbling out of Rocky Valley into the sea.

Benson gave his courageous captain a smile, sharing a mutual sense of security in knowing that the *Rose* was weathering beautifully.

"Surf's up, Mr Benson!"

"So it would appear, sir. So it would appear."

That idea calls for deportment unbecoming a pirate! But the intricate eighth-wave manoeuvre also calls for extraordinary seamanship, and a caravel in the right hands is capable, quite capable thank you, of surfing.

"Here it comes!" announced Ella.

On schedule, it started building – the Mother of All Waves. The wind shrieked its disapproval, its fury, as Benson steered the ship into its teeth.

"On my command, Mr Benson!"

"Standing by, sir."

They were a half mile out, maybe more, close-hauled, when the breaker, reacting to the huge back swell of water fighting its way to the depths, rolled over on itself and knotted with the incoming surge, the *Rose* on its lip.

"Hands to the braces!"

They were prepared – excited fellows all! It wasn't difficult, just adventurous. Rather than ride up and down the ladder as with the previous rollers, Bellamy would mount this monster wind abeam for a few thrilling seconds then gibe. In theory.

"Haul in the for's'l!"

Reality now, not theory. The sail was down in record time; very little canvas is wanted.

"A nice push, I think, Mr Benson."

"Standing by, sir," he said, reconfirming his preparedness.

The ship was slipping sideways across the wave's lip – surfing, so to speak. No roller coaster can match that!

"She has a heart of oak, sir," remarked Mr Pem-David.

"Jettison!" ordered Bellamy.

Heads swivelled round. It was an unusual order! But Benson was ready and yanked the pendant attached to the ship's bell. One resounding peal shattered the storm.

Immediately, the eagle, the one with its wings spread wide, flew from Ezekiel's shoulder and climbed into the sky. There was just enough moonlight to admire the powerful movement of her wings.

"Hard over!"

"Hard over, sir."

The *Rose* glided off the wave's giant back in as gainly a fashion as the giant bird circled the inlet higher and higher. Storm clouds dissipated revealing clear moonlight.

Clang!!! The ship's bell tolled a second time and a giant white fireball enveloped the bird.

A third booming clap echoed off the cliffs. Fire spewed from the eagle's mouth, except now it's no bird at all, rather an immense white dragon. Better yet, a stupendous wyvern – a dragon with legs like an eagle and colossal wings. It, she, continued to circle over land now, higher and higher, fire roaring from her mouth, her flaming eyes staring at Tobit who white-knuckled the rail.

She hovered motionless in the sky as the sturdy ship lifted to the ninth wave.

Time stood still. No yesterdays; no tomorrows; only now. No natural laws, only eternal, supernatural seamlessness.

The dragon swooped over Rocky Valley.

"Hoist the mains'l! Take her in, Mr Benson!"

"Aye aye, sir."

The *Rose* came round as the wind howled yet again. The ocean billowed and rolled forward.

Tobit could see him now; a wispy little fellow underneath a colourless cowl. In his right hand he held a caduceus entwined with two serpents: one red, the other white; natural energies in harmonious balance: one male, the other female.

A bird on Tobit's shoulder replaced the hand that steadied him.

Then it was off! Tobit watched it fly from his shoulder like an arrow; a black bullet bolting toward Merlyn's outstretched arm. Merlyn looked at Tobit, his eyes filled with cosmic mischief. He slammed his staff into the earth as the bird came to rest upon his forearm.

Tobit thought he saw a flash of daylight; blue sky. He was certain of it!

The dragon loosed a blast of fiery breath which tore through the valley and out to sea.

"Heave-to!"

Sails shuddered like thunder. Hot fiery wind rushed across the water and jolted the *Rose* from the ninth wave, which burst into flame and plunged ashore.

The dragon vanished into the valley leaving only a thin trail of ghostly white smoke. The earth rumbled. The wind shifted west of south; Lye Rock was well off the port bow.

"Mr Pem-David, fetch Tobit. All hands, make sail!"

The ship had wind practically abeam where she liked it and pitched evenly over the lesser waves.

"Excellent fresh breeze, Mr Benson."

"Excellent, sir. And fresh, indeed."

"Well done, everyone!" congratulated Bellamy to a round of resounding applause. "Who in Heaven's name are all these people?" he asked.

The quarterdeck was standing room only.

Curious eyes looked to Amos for the answer. "Saints Ninian, Materiana and over there the great Celtic theologian, Pelagius. And there, the Cappadocian Fathers."

"Excuse us! Hellooo?" came a woeful cry from the poop deck.

"Fetch Bran, Mr Pem-David. He's waited a long time."

Merlyn took the new-born child to an elderly monk named Piran who waited by his holy well above the valley. A priest thoughtfully had placed a torch at the well earlier in the evening. A woman was there. She wore a white gown trimmed in blue, in her hand she held a white wand.

When Friar Piran said, "Name this child," Merlyn deferred.

Piran – later named the patron saint of Cornwall

"Arthur. His name is Arthur," she said. Her words floated like feathers upon the lustre of a zillion moonbeams.

Rexque Futurus. Nil desperandum!

Finis

Suggested Reading Bradley, Ian, *The Celtic Way*, Darton, Longman and Todd, London, 1993
Delaney, Frank, *The Celts*, Grafton, London, 1989
Matthews, Caitlin, *The Celtic Book of Days*, Godsfield, 1995
Toynbee, Arnold, *A Study of History*, Oxford, 1946

ACKNOWLEDGEMENTS

Thanks to Ozzie, Andrea, Mary and the staff at Lamorna Pottery, where this book was researched and written, and to Jean Fletcher of the *Matthew* project in Bristol. The cover illustration shows a replica of the *Matthew*, John Cabot's first ship, which is on display in Bristol City Docks.